The

Faggiest Vampire

The
Faggiest Vampire

A Children's Story

written and illustrated by
Carlton Mellick III

SPUNK GOBLIN PRESS

SPUNK GOBLIN PRESS
AN IMPRINT OF ERASERHEAD PRESS

ERASERHEAD PRESS
205 NE BRYANT
PORTLAND, OR 97211

WWW.ERASERHEADPRESS.COM

ISBN: 1-933929-80-4

The Epidemic

9

A mustache epidemic has been sweeping the countryside. And *boy*, what an epidemic it is!

You can't go anywhere these days without seeing mustaches every which way you look. There are strong manly mustaches above the lips of muscular young men and long gray mustaches growing below the noses of elderly old ones. There are thin fancy feminine mustaches on the ladies and soft little children mustaches on the little children.

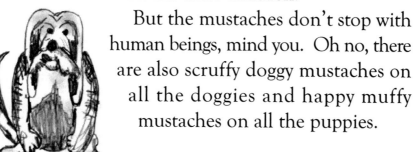

But the mustaches don't stop with human beings, mind you. Oh no, there are also scruffy doggy mustaches on all the doggies and happy muffy mustaches on all the puppies.

Whiskery kitty mustaches grow on kitties, wooly sheep mustaches grow on sheep, and little scaly lizardy mustaches grow on many of the lizards.

There has even been a rumor of some street lamps that have grown lampy mustaches made of pale yellow lights and a toilet that has a toilety mustache made of pink cotton fluff.

10

All of the really smart scientists, and doctors, and wizards, and barbers, and alchemists, and mustachetitions have been working around the clock to figure out the cause of this mustache epidemic. One of the theories is that germs are the cause.

Germs are tiny invisible bugs that get inside your body when you don't wash your hands or talk to people who don't cover their mouths when they cough. When germs get inside your body they make you do strange things. Usually, germs

The Faggiest Vampire

make you cough and sneeze and feel gross and sometimes throw up in the bathroom. But with these germs, you don't cough or feel gross at all. Instead, they make you want to grow a mustache.

At least, that is what all the scientists, doctors, and wizards believe.

CHAINSAW MUSTACHE

BONE MUSTACHE

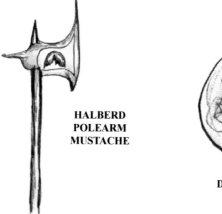

HALBERD POLEARM MUSTACHE

DIMMU BORGIR CD MUSTACHE

11

The Faggy Vampire

12

There is another theory, brought forward by the barbers and the mustachetitions, that this mustache-growing craze is nothing more than a popular fad. They surmise that the source of this fad is likely due to the success of Dargoth Van Gloomfang's signature mustache that has been the talk of the town in recent years. Dargoth is a vampire. He is well known as the faggiest

A MUSTACHETITION

A MUSTACHE WIZARD

vampire in all the land, which makes him one of the most talked-about and celebrated. He is also a connoisseur of fine mustaches. Whether he is responsible for the mustache epidemic or not, nobody is certain. But he sure does have a dandy mustache if I do say so myself.

There are many different types of mustaches. The most common seem to be: handlebar mustaches, taylor mustaches, horseshoe mustaches, toothbrush mustaches, and walrus mustaches. But every so often you'll see some of the more unique and experimental mustaches. I have seen a curly-cue mustache, a braided mustache, a permed mustache, a halved mustache, an arrow mustache, and even something I can only describe as a maniac squid mustache.

13

Dargoth Van Gloomfang has an imperial mustache, which is definitely, in the world of gentleman's mustaches, the most exquisite in existence. It has been around for millennia but is so difficult to grow, so difficult to style and maintain, that it is one of the rarest of them all. But, being immortal, Dargoth has had plenty of time to perfect the art of mustachery.

TYPES OF MUSTACHES

TAYLOR

HORSESHOE

WALRUS

HANDLEBAR

TOOTHBRUSH

CURLY-CUE

PERMED

BRAIDED

FU MANCHU

ARROWS

HALVED

MANIAC SQUID

Mustache Competitions

15

The fun part of all this mustache mischief is that it has encouraged the creation of Mustache Competitions, where everyone can come together and exhibit their fabulous mustaches for medals and prizes. It is very much like a dog show, but for mustaches.

The biggest competition of the season takes place later today, actually. Everyone will be there. From all of the mill workers, to the beautiful ladies, to the rebellious adolescents, to the most sophisticated of socialites. And, of course, all the faggy vampires will be there. A mustache competition just wouldn't be the same without faggy vampires. Especially Dargoth, whose imperial mustache has won best in show every season

since the competitions began.

If you were to see Dargoth's mustache, up close, you would understand how impressive it is. But what a job it is to keep up appearances! Do you know what Dargoth must do to manage such a wonderful mustache? Well, for starters, he must spend most of his day grooming and primping in the most careful way possible. He must do special exercises to maintain the steadiness in his hands and a special mouth workout to maintain the strength of his upper lip.

16

It is very important to keep a strong upper lip when wearing an imperial mustache, otherwise your lip will droop and sag under its weight which will ruin the look of your mustache no matter how well groomed it might be.

And that is just the beginning of Dargoth's grooming duties. There are many more just as tedious rituals, I assure you. Why does he bother with all this complicated facial hair business, you ask? Well, to answer that, I'll have to tell you a little bit more about the man.

Dargoth Van Gloomfang

Dargoth Van Gloomfang lives on a hill high above the village of Gneirwil, in an ancient gothic castle overlooking the Everbleed Sea. He is a portly little vampire, with a fragile hairline, the partially wrinkled eyes of a middle-aged man and the stubby legs of a middle-aged basset hound.

His rotund belly heaves proudly forward as he walks from one wing of his estate to the other,

practicing his courtly posture for the competition that will take place later this evening. Rococo, his faithful human servant with lanky limbs and a blond toothbrush mustache, hurries behind him, measuring the distance between his steps to make sure they are perfectly proportioned down to the millimeter.

18

"Be more nimble, Rococo." Snaps the vampire's pale fingers at the cowering servant, while licking one of his finely-polished vampire fangs. "Your measurements must be absolute perfection!"

Rococo does the best he can, but his best is just never quite good enough to please his picky master.

The Trimmery

19

You see, Dargoth is very particular when it comes to every little thing you can think of. He organizes every single second of his time and expects his plans to be executed exactly to his specifications down to the smallest detail. Rococo is the unfortunate person responsible for making sure Dargoth's day goes as scheduled. It is far from an easy task.

Everyday, as soon as Dargoth wakes up in his ebony coffin at the crack of twilight, which is the time all vampires wake unless they are really lazy vampires with nothing better to do than sleep the night away, Dargoth immediately goes into his castle's trimmery for his daily mustache trimming. The trimmery is a small room in the third basement of the north-

east tower designed to keep all drafts of wind far away during the grooming process. It is filled with rows and rows of mirrors (the kind vampires can see themselves in) of varying degrees of magnification. He expects Rococo to be waiting for him in the trimmery with everything perfectly organized according to his specifications.

20

His assortment of mustache combs must be placed in a symmetrical arch (which Dargoth calls his comb rainbow) around the center of the grooming table, separated .85 of an inch. His mustache waxes, conditioners, and scented oils must be placed on the left side of the comb rainbow and his wallet

of mustache scissors must be set on the right of the comb rainbow. Each of the scissors in his kit has a different shape and function. One is for cutting the bottom of his mustache above the lips, another is for snipping around the cheeks, another is for maneuvering around the nostrils. Actually, there are so many of them with so many specific functions that it will boggle your mind if I explain any more than that.

Rococo himself must also be situated in his assigned position as his master enters. He is not to blink or move a muscle until after Dargoth sits down in his trimming chair and removes his mustache net.

By the way, the mustache net (also known as a snood) is the most important item in maintaining a gentleman's mustache. It looks very much like a hair net, except it is built for mustaches. It must be worn during sleep, during brisk jogs, on windy days, while traveling by train or coach, while playing cricket or polo, and sometimes while levitating (depending on how rapid of a levitation it is), in order to make certain that gravity and pressure do not pervert the shape of the mustache.

Dargoth also has a waterproof mustache cap

for bathing, swimming, and rainy nights, but he doesn't keep one in his trimmery. After Dargoth places his snood in the center of the rainbow, he gets to work, cutting and combing and waxing and molding. Rococo, meanwhile, must stand there patiently while his master sculpts, handing him tools as they are called for. During this very, very long and painstaking process, Rococo must not create any wind with his limbs, yet he

22

must be lightning-quick when assisting his master. He is also only allowed to breathe once per minute and it must only be the shallowest of breaths.

This is a very stressful time for poor Rococo, and it is by far his least favorite part of the day.

Rococo's Party Hats

24

Rococo's most favorite part of the day comes after his master's mustache trimming.

As soon as he leaves the trimmery, Dargoth likes to go straight to his observatory and admire his mustache in the light of the moon. He lounges there for an entire hour, mirror in hand, inhaling steamy snifters of spiced pear brandy. He, of course, does not sip the brandy. He just likes to let the steam rise through the hairs of his mustache and enter his nostrils. It's a little nightly ritual that puts him at peace with the universe.

And, since he wishes to be at peace, he allows

Rococo an hour of time off. This is the only break Rococo is allowed during his master's waking hours, so he uses his free time very wisely.

Everyday during this break, Rococo rushes across the estate to his quarters in the south wing. He leaps his long pogo-stick legs into his hobby bench and gets right to work. What Rococo works on is the thing that makes him happiest in life. He is one of those people who believes you should always do what makes you happiest in life, whenever your work is through. No, he doesn't play with jump-ropes or toy trains. What makes Rococo happiest is decorating party hats.

26

He decorates one a day, with glue and glitter and multi-colored tissue paper. He makes them as colorful as possible and gives each one a special ornament. Sometimes he will design a ladybug ornament for the front of a hat, other times he will give a hat ears like a bunny or teddy bear ears. He also likes to glue little objects to the hats that he finds around the village, like a dried daisy or a tiny doll head.

Why does this man have such a passion for decorating hats? Your guess is as good as mine. Since Rococo doesn't have any friends, he has never

told anybody about his passion. So nobody knows. But, boy, if you were to see him when he gets into making party hats, you'd hardly recognize the fellow. His smile stretches so wide across his face that the corners of his lips nearly touch the corners of his eyebrows.

He has been working on these hats day after day, year after year, for so long that they are stacked all the way to the ceiling against every wall in his room.

27

Someday I bet he will make so many hats that he won't even have enough space in his room to construct any more of them. Now, won't that be a funny predicament!

The Haberdashery

28

Due to the mustache competition, today's schedule is exceptionally strict and rigorous, so Rococo is not even allowed his hour break to decorate party hats. In fact, Dargoth must have forgotten that there are only twenty-four hours in a day, because he has scheduled thirty-seven hours of work into today's activities. Unless time stands still for awhile, there will be no way for them to get through all of Dargoth's plans.

They have finally finished perfecting the vampire's walk for the competition and now it is time to perfect his outfit of the evening, so they are heading down to the village for a visit to the local haberdashery.

If Rococo's passion is decorating party hats,

The Faggiest Vampire

then Dargoth's passion is going to the haberdashery. There is nothing that makes him more happy and excited. Haberdasheries are shops that specialize in fancy clothing accessories. You will find luxuriant ribbons and graceful capes, elegant gloves and grandiloquent buttons, ornate ties and dignified pink ascots.

     Whenever Dargoth is in the haberdashery he prances around on the tips of his toes, shouting across the room at his man servant, "Oh, look at this! This is absolutely delectable!" And then he giggles under his perky mustache.

29

     Rococo drives Dargoth in his gloomy vampire coach down the hill into Gneirwil. It is a black coach with dim lanterns, gargoyle adornments, and spider

webs painted onto the side. Dargoth is in the back, wearing a travel-snood on his mustache and filing his long black nails into perfect points.

30

The citizens gather in the street to watch him pass. They pretend to cower as he passes, to show their respect and admiration. In reciprocation, Dargoth reveals a single vampire tooth and raises a pointy eyebrow to show his appreciation for their tribute.

When they arrive at the haberdashery, Dargoth just can't maintain his sophisticated poise any longer and leaps out of the coach before Rococo can open the door for him. Then he skitters sideways like a vampire-shaped crab into the shop.

Dargoth immediately discovers something new and wonderful.

"Oh my, a diaphanous gossamer!" he says to Rococo who is still outside parking the coach. "It's absolutely recherché!" His giggles echo through the moonlit streets.

Rococo already has no idea what his master is talking about. He knows that when he gets in this mood it is best to just stay out of his way, so Rococo decides to wait outside with the coach and breathe in the fresh Broodsarrow air.

Broodsarrow

Oh dear, I've forgotten to tell you all about the setting of our faggy story! I must apologize, but do understand that I can easily get carried away with all this talk of vampires and mustaches.

This story is set in a place called The Land of Broodsarrow. It is a region far away from our modern world of gizmos and technology. It is a place built for vampires who wish to reside in an old world setting, where things are kept exactly as they were centuries ago.

You see, vampires live for a very long time. And when people live for a very long time they get so used to the way things are that they don't want anything to change. Change is a scary thing to them, just like ghosts and graveyards are scary to you and me. Perhaps you have a grandma or a grumpy neigh-

bor who often talks of the good old days? This is because they wish things could go back to the way they used to be, before things started to change on them.

32

The Faggiest Vampire

Well, most vampires, such as Dargoth Van Gloomfang, are far older than your grandma and even your grumpy next door neighbor. In fact, I bet Dargoth is ten or twenty times older than your grandma and neighbor combined! So that makes them absolutely terrified of change and makes them want, more than anything, to go back to their good old days.

33

That is why Broodsarrow was created. It is a place where things remain just as they used to be, centuries ago, when the vampires were young. And nothing ever changes here. The technology never changes. The people never change. The styles of art and music never change. The seasons don't even change!

That's right, even the season is frozen in time here in Broodsarrow. It is forever late autumn, which is every vampire's favorite time of year. They like it because it is rainy and gloomy and the sun rarely ever shines. Even though vampires sleep during the day, they still don't like the sun to ever shine. Sunlight doesn't actually turn vampires into ash, as many people believe, but it does put them in a very grumpy mood.

Rococo, on the other hand, quite enjoys the

sunlight on the rare occasions that the sun makes an appearance. He, like all humans in Broodsarrow, has lived his entire life in this land and knows nothing of the faraway world that we are from. He doesn't know that there is such a thing as summer, where sunlight is very common and makes everyone very happy.

34

Humans are not allowed to like sunlight in Broodsarrow. They are also not allowed to let anything change. But Rococo can't help but enjoy himself in the sunlight and is sad that he can't express this joy to anyone else. He can, however, show his appreciation for the moonlight, which he also enjoys.

Right now, while his master is in the shop, Rococo takes his time soaking in the moonlight and breathing in the fresh air.

But something ruins his moment in mid fresh air breath. A group of shadowy figures are floating past him towards the haberdashery.

Rococo gasps as he recognizes the face of the lead figure. It is none other than Baron Van Ravengraves, Dargoth's greatest rival.

Baron Van Ravengraves

Baron Van Ravengraves is the new vampire on the block. He is young, hip, a tad on the rebellious side, and some even say that he may have Dargoth beat as the faggiest vampire in all of Broodsarrow.

This vampire emits such a grand amount of fagginess that one cannot help but be completely overwhelmed by his presence. He likes to walk (or float) down the street, wearing his dark sunglasses and black muscle shirt tucked into scuffed blue jeans. His shiny leather trenchcoat blows in the wind as he smooths back his Leonardo Dicaprio haircut. He's completely saturated from head to toe with coolness, and fagginess.

Unlike Dargoth, he doesn't travel with a hu-

man servant. No, Baron has no need of servants. He travels with his own vampire entourage. His posse follows him around wherever he goes, wearing the same sunglasses and trenchcoats (only theirs are a little less shiny). Though they are not as faggy as their leader, they too exude an intense amount of fagginess.

36

There is Lars Van Broadchin, a muscular Scandinavian with a shaved head and an enormous tribal tattoo that stretches up his neck and across the left side of his face.

There is Tooth Van Bladeblood, a tall black vampire with a Wesley Snipes haircut. He carries a samurai sword and never speaks.

There is Rain Van Razorwind, a female vampire with very long straight black hair and black lipstick. She is perhaps the faggiest of Baron's entourage because she's written a book of ethereal poetry.

And then there is Doomstorm, their vampire bulldog with a spiked leather collar.

The five of them live together in Ravengraves Castle, which was recently built next door to Dargoth Castle. All night and even into the next day sometimes, these hooligans throw loud parties that disrupt the peaceful ambiance of Gneirwil. They

have no respect for the elder vampires and even inspire *change*. The only reason they are able to get away with all of this is because they are just so darned faggy that everyone likes them. They can do pretty much anything they want.

Baron Van Ravengraves is not a conventional vampire. He has lived most of his life outside of Broodsarrow in the modern fast-paced world of Los Angeles, California. Only recently has he decided to rejoin the vampire community, but he seems to have brought his fast-paced lifestyle with him. This has put Dargoth's methodical life into complete disarray.

38

Dargoth doesn't like Baron one bit. Not only is Baron chaotic and untraditional, but he is also trying to steal Dargoth's position as the faggiest vampire in all of Broodsarrow. The two of them can't be in the same place at the same time or Dargoth's face will wrinkle into an angry red ball and his mustache hairs will stand on end.

Rococo knows this. That is why he is running into the haberdashery to warn Dargoth of the coming Ravengraves.

Dargoth in Trouble

But Rococo is too late!

As Baron enters the haberdashery, Dargoth is on his way out with his newly purchased clothing (a diaphanous gossamer and a silver-glittered ascot). They run into each other face to face and old Dargoth Van Gloomfang is filled with such shock that his eyebrows raise so high on his forehead that they seem to float off into midair above his face.

"Excuse me!" Dargoth snaps at the brood.

"Well, well," says Ravengraves. "If it isn't old Gloomfang . . ."

The young vampire whips his sunglasses off of his face for dramatic effect.

Dargoth's mouth drops open as he sees something

different about young Baron. It is very small, perhaps an illusion, but there seems to be a line of hair just above his lips. Dargoth steps in closer to get a better look. Yes, it is a line of hair. It is a mustache! A pencil mustache, to be exact. But this is the thinnest pencil mustache Dargoth has ever seen.

40

A pencil mustache is a very thin mustache that grows just above the lip. They are so thin, in fact, that they appear to be drawn onto the face with a pencil. It is very hard to style a pencil mustache because they are so fine and delicate. If you are not careful while trimming, you could end up shaving the whole mustache off without realizing it.

Dargoth has never been able to grow a proper pencil mustache. He has tried and failed. You see, he might have the refined steady hands required to shave facial hair into a pencil mustache, but Dargoth's facial skin is just too rough and rugged. His pencil mustaches come out bumpy and squiggly and crude. They are so embarrassing that they must be shaved off immediately before anyone gets the chance to see. Yet, here Baron is with a pencil mustache. This unsophisticated brute. And not only is it a great pencil mustache, it is the greatest Dargoth has ever seen. It is so thin, so fine, that it doesn't

The Faggiest Vampire

just look pencil-thin . . . it looks razor-thin. You can't even see it unless you are standing right up close to his face.

Just like there has never been a vampire faggy enough to rival the fagginess of Dargoth, no mustache has ever been elegant enough to rival the imperial mustache of Dargoth. This has all come as a major shock. Dargoth can hardly keep his shopping bags in his hands as the anger builds in his brain.

"That mustache is divine!" Dargoth says, not able to contain himself. "You better not be entering that in the mustache competition!"

Ravengraves puts his sunglasses back on and says, "What? Afraid you'll lose, Gloomfang?"

"I never lose!" Dargoth says.

"Own up, Gloomfang," says Ravengraves. "You're yesterday's news. Nobody cares about you or your tired old man mustache anymore. I'm the new hotness in town. I'm going to win that competition. Then everyone in Broodsarrow will know that I'm the faggiest of all faggy vampires once and for all."

Dargoth's mouth frowns so loudly at the young vampires that it makes his mustache groan.

"I have been the faggiest of all faggy vampire

for ages," Dargoth says. "There is no way you can change that."

"Change is coming," Ravengraves says, "after I win the mustache competition." His boys, Lars and Tooth, high-five each other as he says that.

Dargoth raises an eyebrow and tries to calm himself.

42

"Your pencil mustache is good," he says. "I'll give you that. But it's not as good as mine. There is no way that a pencil mustache, even one as fine as yours, can ever defeat an imperial mustache."

Ravengraves rips his sunglasses off of his face again, even more dramatically than before. He disappears into a puff of smoke and then reappears behind Dargoth's shoulder.

He whispers into the older vampire's ear, "We'll see about that."

Then Ravengraves snaps his fingers at his entourage and they follow him out of the haberdashery, into the foggy night.

Bat Time

43

Dargoth is back at his castle. He has turned himself into a bat and is fluttering around the ballroom. Whenever Dargoth is stressed or worried about something, he turns himself into a bat to cheer himself up. Well, not his entire body. He doesn't like to turn his head into a bat head because it messes up his mustache, so right now he is a flying human head with bat wings instead of ears.

Normally, this is one of Dargoth's favorite things to do. He likes to flutter through the streets of Gneirwil exposing his finely-polished fangs to people walking down the sidewalks.

Dargoth doesn't drink human blood. It is not a very dignified thing to do in Broodsarrow

nowadays. Plus, he wouldn't want to dirty his gentleman's mustache with gross gooey blood, now would he?

But there is something about the hunt that makes a vampire's life more thrilling, so Dargoth still goes out in the middle of the night in bat form (I mean head-with-bat-wings form) and hunts for a human victim. When he finds human victims he doesn't drink their blood. Instead, he swoops down right in front of their faces and wiggles his mustache at them.

This is normally a shock to his human victims, but they rarely ever scream. They tend to laugh and smile and wave at Dargoth's floating head and wiggling mustache. It makes them feel special and happy that he would choose them as victims. They are also thankful that Dargoth is such a nice vampire, and would never drink any of their blood.

But Dargoth doesn't like them to laugh at him. They are supposed to be scared. Victims shouldn't have fun being victims, should they? Whenever Dargoth is feeling especially fragile and can't handle being laughed at, he just flutters around his ballroom during bat time.

Sometimes, if he feels like going on a hunt for

44

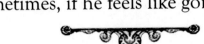

a victim, he will flutter through the dark corridors of the castle and swoop down on Rococo when he least expects. He will wiggle his mustache and Rococo will scream and pretend to act really frightened by his master's attack. Rococo knows how sensitive his master can be, so he never giggles or laughs at him when he wiggles his mustache.

Right now Dargoth is not using his bat time to hunt down a victim. Instead, he is using it to think. Flying around in bat form is good for helping you think. Dargoth is trying to figure out what he is going to do about Baron Van Ravengraves, who has threatened to steal his status as faggiest vampire.

Should he just do his best and hope that his best is enough to defeat Ravengraves? This is what you or I would do if we were faced with a situation such as this, but Dargoth is not that type of vampire. Winning every mustache competition, and being the faggiest of all faggy vampires, is so important to Dargoth that he must do everything in his power to assure that his success is certain.

So Dargoth flutters in circles around his ballroom, crafting a devious plan to sabotage the fagginess of Baron Van Ravengraves.

Rococo's Work in Progress

47

While his master is in bat-form, Rococo has some time to slip away and work on decorating party hats. He has not had the chance to decorate a party hat all day and it would be just the thing to cheer him up during such a stressful period.

He doesn't think he has much time to construct an entirely new hat, but he does have time to add touches to his work-in-progress. His face widens into a big smile as he takes a box out from under his bed and places it onto his table. Inside, is his work-in-progress. It is the hat that is going to be his masterpiece.

He has been working on this particular hat for

a very long time. He wants it to be perfect. That is because this party hat is the one he is making for Dargoth Van Gloomfang. It must be very special, because Dargoth is so picky when it comes to gifts. And he does so want his master to love it, because Dargoth is the closest thing to a friend Rococo has ever had in his life.

The party hat is designed with fancy ribbons and fabrics that Rococo purchased (with his own money!) at the haberdashery. They are organized in a very symmetrical and eye-pleasing fashion that he knows Dargoth will appreciate. And, don't forget, every party hat comes with a special ornament! Constructing the special ornament for this very special party hat is the part that has been taking Rococo so long. What Rococo has been constructing is a life-sized imperial mustache made out of the tiny trimmings of Dargoth's real life mustache.

And what a project that is! Each day, after Dargoth's twilight trimming, Rococo picks up every little miniature hair from the floor of the trimmery and collects them into a bag. Then he takes those hairs to his work-in-progress and adds them to the imperial mustache ornament on Dargoth's party hat.

The Faggiest Vampire

It will all be worth the effort to Rococo once he sees Dargoth's reaction to the hat. While working, Rococo likes to imagine what his master's reaction will be when he finally gets to see this party hat. It will surely be a grand reaction. Dargoth will leap up in the air with joy, just as he does when he finds something he likes at the haberdashery.

This will make Rococo happier than he has ever been in his entire life.

Right now, Rococo can't stop smiling as he imagines what it must be like to be happier than he has ever been in his entire life.

The hat is very close to completion, but Rococo must make sure every tiny hair is styled perfectly. He doesn't want to be hasty. He is sure Dargoth will just love it, even as it is now, but he must make sure every detail is exactly right before presenting it to his master.

The Sunglasses Heist

50

Dargoth's plan to sabotage Baron's fagginess is simple: he plans to steal all of his sunglasses.

That would put a damper on Baron's plans. Without being able to take off his sunglasses for dramatic effect, Baron loses a huge amount of fagginess. It might just be enough to take him out of the running for faggiest vampire.

Dargoth and Rococo sneak across the hillside in the moonlight. They creep with arched backs and tiny steps as they approach the back entrance of Ravengraves Castle.

Baron and his gang are throwing yet another late night party. There is loud music playing and many people in attendance, both human and vam-

pire. Many of the humans and vampires are dressed in blue jeans and leather trenchcoats, mimicking Baron's look.

"He influences too much change!" Dargoth whispers to Rococo when he sees the party guests inside. "These articles of clothing should not be worn by the citizens of Broodsarrow!"

Once inside, the two elegantly dressed bandits tip-toe past the party and upstairs to the sunglasses pantry. There is a large supply of sunglasses here in the sunglasses pantry. There are hundreds of them, all the exact same style. Baron must have brought so many into Broodsarrow because he knew that they don't sell them here. This way he will never run out, no matter how many he breaks or lends out to his friends.

"How will we carry all of those?" Rococo asks.

"Hmm . . ." Dargoth scratches his first chin. "We can't steal them all. We'll have to just break them here."

"Won't that be a lot of breaking?" Rococo asks.

"Hmm . . ." Dargoth scratches his second chin. "Yes. We will have to break quickly."

And break quickly is what they do. Starting with the sunglasses on the top shelf and working

their way down to the ones on the bottom shelf, they break sunglasses left and right. They stomp them under their shoes, they snap them into halves, they pop out the lenses and bend the frames out of shape.

When they are through, not a single pair of sunglasses is left intact. Now the pantry is just rows and rows of twisted, warped black pieces of plastic.

"Won't Baron be surprised next time he tries to put on a pair of sunglasses," Dargoth says. "He'll probably never want to show his sunglassesless face in public ever again!"

53

With that, Dargoth and Rococo sneak out the way they came in, but not before running into one of Baron's entourage.

Rain Van Razorwind is outside baying at the moon. Unlike most vampires, Rain doesn't turn into a bat when she's on the hunt. She turns into a white wolf. Yes, it is rare, but sometimes vampires prefer the shapes of wolves, or rats, or snakes, or even black rabbits over the shape of the bat.

So when Dargoth and Rococo see this white wolf, they don't know it is Rain at all. They think it is just an ordinary wolf basking in the moonlight, as ordinary wolves tend to do. But Rain has spotted

them and she knows that they have been up to no good, sneaking around as they are.

As soon as the two intruders leave the property, Rain changes back into human form and goes upstairs to find the sunglasses pantry has been broken into. When she shows Baron, and Lars, and Tooth, and Doomstorm, they all grow very sad. They look at the sunglasses as if all of their toys have been broken.

54

They vow that Dargoth Van Gloomfang will not get away with what he has done. He will pay for causing them such grief.

Wimpire

Ravengraves and his entourage get back at Dargoth by sneaking into his house and damaging some clothing accessories that they know he holds dear.

They spray-paint the word "wimpire" on his expensive new diaphanous gossamer and his silver-glittered ascot, both of which he planned to wear during the mustache competition. "This is an outrage!" Dargoth cries to his defiled clothing accessories. "How can they deface such beauty? Don't they know art when they see it?"

He paces back and forth in his dressing room and says, "To take revenge on me, this I understand. But to deface such fine clothing, that is just unconscionable!"

Rococo waits in the doorway, not sure what he can do to console his master. Dargoth did this to

himself, remember. He should have known that when you do something nasty to someone else, they will most likely do something just as nasty back to you.

Dargoth reads the word painted on his clothes. "Wimpire? What does that mean? Are they saying that I go on *wims*? I do not go on wims! They are trying to slander my good name!"

Rococo clears his throat.

56

The Faggiest Vampire

"I don't think they mean *whims*, sir," he says. "I think they mean to call you a wimpy vampire. Wimpire being a shortened, slang-like version of the insult."

"Wimpire!" screams Dargoth. "I'll show them who's a wimpire!"

Dargoth changes into bat form and storms out of the room. He goes back to fluttering in circles down in the ballroom, so that he can craft another devious plan to get back at Baron for ruining his new clothes. It doesn't occur to him that whatever nasty thing he does to Baron next, Baron will most likely pay him back by doing something doubly nasty. And then Dargoth will have to scheme up another revenge, which will be reciprocated, and on and on, until it ends really badly.

All wars end really badly.

57

Rococo's Secret

58

Now that Dargoth is doing his bat routine again, Rococo decides to go back to his room to work on perfecting his work-in-progress.

But this time Dargoth has devised a scheme very quickly and just as soon as Rococo places the mustachioed party hat onto his work table the door to his room bursts open.

Dargoth, being a noble gentleman, has always respected the privacy of his servant's quarters. But tonight the vampire has become exceedingly moody and charges into Rococo's room with disregard.

"Where have you been?" Dargoth cries. "I have urgent need of you!"

Rococo usually leaps to attention when

called on by his master, but now he is too busy hiding his unfinished party hat with his arms to stand upright.

His master notices something odd about the way Rococo is acting. He can tell something really suspicious is going on. He looks around the room for something suspicious and, to his surprise, he discovers stacks and stacks of colorful party hats piled all the way to the ceiling.

59

"What might I ask are these?" Dargoth asks.

Rococo's voice shakes. "Please, I never meant for you to see them . . ."

"But what are they?"

"They are my secrets," Rococo says.

"Secrets?" Dargoth shouts. "They look like crudely designed party hats!"

"Yes, party hats," Rococo says, softly. "I decorate them in my spare time."

Dargoth laughs. "Why on Earth would you decorate party hats?"

"It makes me happy," Rococo responds.

Dargoth paces around the tiny room, examining all of the crazy childish hats. They have interested Dargoth so much that he has almost forgotten why he needed Rococo in the first place.

"How can decorating party hats possibly make you happy?" Dargoth asks.

"Because . . ." Rococo begins, shrinking in his seat with a face like a puppy dog. "Someday, if I ever have a birthday party, I like to think of how happy it will make all of my guests if I give them these fun hats to wear."

60

Dargoth bursts into laughter. "Party? Guests? You are forty-three years old and you have never once had a birthday party! How on earth could you still be hopeful of having one now? You don't even have any friends!"

Dargoth continues laughing. He laughs so hard that his round belly jiggles and his mustache wiggles.

"You have hundreds of hats here," Dargoth continues. "To fill all of these hats you would have to get every single person in town to come to your party! Nobody even knows who you are!"

Dargoth is being particularly rude to his servant this evening. Having his clothing accessories ruined has put him in the worst of moods. Not only is he acting rude, but he's become downright mean.

"*Somebody* knows who I am," Rococo says.

"Do tell!" Dargoth cries. "Who is this person who actually knows who you are?"

"You," Rococo says.

The servant picks up the almost-finished party hat and shows it to his master.

"I made this one special for you," he says.

Before Rococo can tell him about how difficult of a process it has been to make this hat, how many hours he has spent perfecting it, how proud he is of it, Dargoth plucks the thing out of his hand and crumples it up without even looking at it.

61

"Nevermind," Dargoth says, tossing the crumpled hat over his shoulder. "We don't have time for anymore of this. There is important work to be done."

Rococo stares at his crumpled masterpiece, his mouth wide in horror. It is as if all of his hopes and dreams were crushed right there in front of him. Everything that made him happy and cheerful, gone. Everything that made his life worth living, gone. Because of that one insensitive act.

His master snaps his fingers and Rococo, not knowing what else to do, follows obediently.

Bulldog Abduction

62

Remember when I said that Dargoth had scheduled thirty-seven hours of work into today's activities even though there are only twenty-four hours in a day? Well, I have just realized that he did that on purpose. Not because he forgot how many hours were in a day, but because he decided to combine two days into one.

That's right, Dargoth and Rococo plan to stay up all day preparing for the competition without getting any sleep at all. Since they will be awake during the day, when all other vampires are asleep, Dargoth plans to send Rococo over to Ravengraves Castle to do something horrible in order to sabotage his rival's fagginess.

The Faggiest Vampire

What Dargoth has in mind is so cruel and un-called for that Rococo must take a deep breath just to be sure he heard his master correctly. Dargoth wants him to sneak over to Ravengraves Castle and kidnap Doomstorm, their vampire bulldog.

Doomstorm is the mascot of this brood of vampires, and Dargoth believes that their spirits will be broken if they lose this mascot. They will become sick with worry and one cannot be confident with one's fagginess when sick with worry. He wants Rococo to take the bulldog far away from Ravengraves Castle and tie him to a tree. Once Baron realizes his pet bulldog is missing, he will be so worried that he will even go out in the daylight to search for him. By the time he finds Doomstorm, far away from home, he will have spent so much time in the sun that he will be the grumpiest vampire in all of Broodsarrow for at least a week. And a grumpy vampire can never be the faggiest vampire.

The plan is simple enough. Executing it, on the other hand, might be a different story.

Faggy Coffins

64

Rococo treks across the hillside to Ravengraves Castle. The morning sun is shining in the sky, a rare treat for Rococo, but it still doesn't cheer him up after his master's betrayal.

Since Baron Van Ravengraves doesn't employ the services of human caretakers, and there are no vampire hunters in The Land of Broodsarrow, Rococo is free to enter the castle through the front gate without creeping around back. He walks right down the long shadowy staircase leading into their crypt and locates the five faggy coffins containing the five faggy vampires.

It is not a very stylish crypt and they are not very stylish coffins. They are more like rugged

The Faggiest Vampire

wooden crates than coffins, but they can still be considered pretty faggy just because Baron and his gang are using them.

65

    Dargoth's crypt, on the other hand, is the most luxuriant in the land. It is more like a throne room than a crypt, filled with red velvet draperies and 12-piece candelabras. His giant ebony coffin is decorated with blood-red roses and a bronze bust of a younger more handsome Dargoth Van Gloomfang. There are classical works of art hanging on the walls and mellow harpsichord music playing in the background. When his servant enters in the twilight to wake his master from his daily slumber, a vent opens in the eastern wall that releases dozens of tiny black butterflies that flutter around the room like dark

dancing flower petals in the moonlight.

Baron's crypt is more about being practical than elegant. These coffins are so lightweight that they can be taken on road trips without much effort. Dargoth could never do that with his enormous ebony coffin.

66

Due to the varying sizes of the coffins, Rococo has no problem finding Doomstorm's. It is the squarish bulldog-sized coffin on the end. When Rococo opens the lid, he sees Doomstorm fast asleep with his vampire teeth sticking out from behind his jowls.

The vampire bulldog snores loudly. He doesn't wake up or stop snoring as Rococo lifts him out of his coffin and wraps him up in a dusty shroud. Though very heavy for the gangly man, Rococo is able to carry Doomstorm upstairs and out of the castle without much difficulty.

These vampires had been up partying all night, so they must all be in the deepest slumbers. Not a single one of them notices Rococo as he sneaks away with their mascot.

Doomstorm's Revenge

67

Well, even though this vampire bulldog has been up partying all night, he is not in the deepest of sleeps. It isn't long before he stops snoring and takes a look around, wondering why he is not lying comfy in his coffin as he should be.

Rococo gets him halfway across the hillside when the bulldog starts to growl and struggle to get away. The servant holds onto him as tight as he can, but bulldogs are tough. Especially vampire bulldogs. Doomstorm pushes off of Rococo's chest with his stubby legs and breaks out of the servant's grasp.

But Doomstorm doesn't run back to his coffin right away, as other vampire dogs might do. You see, bulldogs are the grumpiest dogs in the whole world.

And if you take a vampire bulldog out of his snugly coffin while he is having a most delightful snooze, then bring the vampire bulldog out into the bright sunlight, you get without a doubt *the* most grumpy creature that you could ever possibly lay eyes on.

And what do grumpy bulldogs do to people that make them angry? That's right, they bite them as hard as they can right on the butt.

That is exactly what Doomstorm does to Rococo, but since Doomstorm is a vampire bulldog his teeth are long and sharp and the bite hurts three times more than a normal bulldog bite.

68

As Rococo stands there crying and rubbing his wounded bottom, Doomstorm struts off proudly into the forest to return to his comfortable little coffin in Ravengraves Crypt.

Do not Disturb the slumber of Doom StorM

Dargoth in Trouble

When Rococo returns to Dargoth Castle, his master is very angry about the failure of his mission.

"I will have to handle this myself," Dargoth says.

Rococo helps dress him in clothing that will protect him from the daylight. He covers every inch of his skin with two layers of thick dark clothing. He gives him airtight gloves to wear, a long cloak with a very deep hood that covers him like a blanket, a dark veil to put over his face, a lovely black parasol to hold over his head, and a vacuum-sealed triple-strength sun-blocking ultra-snood to protect his mustache from the sunlight.

What a ridiculous sight this little vampire

is in such an outfit!

Dargoth looks in the mirror and scratches his chin.

He says, "I wish there was something I could wear over my eyes to protect my vision from the sunlight, something similar to spectacles but with tinted lenses . . ."

"Oh well," Dargoth says. "I guess such a thing just doesn't exist in Broodsarrow . . ."

70

The vampire goes out into the daylight by himself. It is the first time in several decades that he has had a need to leave his home during the daytime. He steps carefully towards Ravengraves Castle. It is very difficult for Dargoth to maneuver in his outfit and even more difficult for him to see where he is stepping, so he must proceed with utmost caution. For, if he were to fall, he might lose his hood or his parasol and might get a glimpse of the bright sunlight. Just one glimpse of the sun and Dargoth would surely be grumpy for the rest of the day, causing him to lose not only the mustache competition but his reputation as faggiest vampire.

Once he gets to Ravengraves Castle, he marches straight down to the crypt and goes right to the side of Baron's coffin. Now, I have to tell you that Dargoth just isn't himself today. He has lost all sen-

sibility. When someone such as Dargoth loses his sensibility, he commits a desperate act.

The desperate act Dargoth is committing is almost too heinous for me to mention. I really wish I could tell you that Dargoth opens Baron's coffin lid and, instead of doing anything nasty, he gives him a friendly letter that explains how sorry he is for the grief he has caused and that he would love for the two of them to become wonderful friends. But that's just not how this story goes.

71

After Dargoth opens the lid to Baron's coffin, he pulls out a shaving razor and . . . shaves Baron's pencil mustache right off of his face! Baron partied especially hard last night, harder than usual, so he does not wake up while his mustache is shaved. Then, with a black makeup pencil, Dargoth draws a new pencil mustache on Baron's face exactly where the old one used to be.

Dargoth smiles proudly at his job well done. The judges at tonight's competition will undeniably spot this drawn-on mustache as a fake and he will be disqualified. Not only will Baron lose the competition, but his reputation as a faggy vampire will be tarnished forever! Because cheating is not a very faggy thing to do.

The Consequence of Dirty Deeds

72

As soon as Dargoth returns to his castle, he begins to regret what he has done. He finally realizes how terrible he has been to poor Baron. Nobody deserves to have their mustache shaved off, especially such a fine mustache as Baron's pencil mustache.

Dargoth puts himself in Baron's shoes and thinks about how horrible it would be if someone were to shave off his imperial mustache. It would be absolutely devastating! He could handle being only the second most faggy vampire in Broodsarrow, but he just couldn't handle losing his beloved mustache. His mustache is his love, his life.

His eyes pop out of his head as a thought

occurs to him.

"What if Baron wants to get revenge by shaving off *my* mustache?" he cries.

Now he is beginning to understand why he never should have started such a nasty feud with his next door neighbor.

"No, that must not happen!"

He tries to console himself.

"Baron is a hooligan, but he surely must be a reasonable vampire," Dargoth says to himself. "He knows how important my mustache is to me. He knows that it is the thing that makes my life worth living. He knows that without my mustache all of my hopes and dreams will be crushed . . ."

73

He droops dramatically into the shadows of his castle and says, "Surely, no one is so cruel as to destroy that which I hold so dear . . ."

Then Dargoth remembers what he did to Rococo and his party hat. He realizes that he, himself, has destroyed the thing that his servant held so dear. He crushed Rococo's dreams without a second thought, and Rococo is someone he is rather fond of. Baron is not fond of Dargoth at all, so he certainly will not hesitate to remove his imperial mustache.

"This is terrible!" cries the faggy vampire.

Dargoth spends the entire day worrying about this. He just knows Baron will be coming for him soon to collect his mustache. He worries so much, in fact, that he doesn't even notice all of the hairs falling out of his mustache and piling up on his big round belly.

74

Rococo's Toothbrush Mustache

Rococo is sitting in his quarters, trying not to look at the crumpled party hat on the floor. Now that his dreams have been crushed he is terribly sad. Rococo doesn't like to be sad. He prefers to be happy. Rococo is one of those people who believes you should always try to be happy even when everything seems to be very sad.

So Rococo decides to pick up a new hobby, one that will not only make him happy but also one that his master will respect. It is difficult to have a hobby that Dargoth will respect, because the only hobby Dargoth is known to respect is the

grooming of mustaches.

Perhaps that is it. Perhaps Rococo should develop a deeper passion in maintaining his mustache. As I mentioned at the beginning of this story, Rococo has a bright blond toothbrush mustache. It is not a very fancy mustache, but it is one that Rococo knows how to keep nice. A toothbrush mustache is as wide as the bristly section of a toothbrush. From a distance, it sometimes doesn't look like a mustache at all. It basically looks like a square-shaped patch of fur lingering below the nostrils.

Rococo likes the toothbrush mustache because it is square. He likes to think that his square mustache makes his master happy, since his master is so fond of straight, even lines.

"Yes," Rococo says to himself in the mirror, taking out his crude secondhand mustache grooming tools. "I will start taking pride in mustache grooming."

He combs his little mustache with a little mustache comb. His blond mustache hairs are very straight and easy to maintain.

"Perhaps I might even enter the mustache competition," he says. "Maybe I'll even get an honorable mention award in the toothbrush category!"

76

The Big Day

77

Night falls on the quiet little town of Gnei-rwil. In the town square, by the old church and courthouse, bustling activity blooms as the biggest mustache festival of the season opens its gates to the general public.

All of the contestants in the mustache competition have already taken their places in booths lining the perimeter of the square. Men, women, children, grandpas and babies fill the sidewalks and gray lawns. They buy cotton candy and toasted apples from food vendors, then tour the exhibits to see all the wonderful mustaches on display. The spectators take their time viewing every single mustache, admiring the details and complexities of these finely

crafted facial hairdos. Though they take their time studying each and every contestant's entry, everyone is most excited to see the majestic imperial mustache of the returning champion.

Dargoth Van Gloomfang already has accumulated a massive crowd around his booth. He perches like a noble eagle, his neck stretched forward and tilted slightly to show his mustache at the perfect angle. On the outside, he looks calm and composed. His posture is spot-on. But, on the inside, Dargoth is a nervous wreck. He knows that Baron Van Ravengraves is plotting against him. He knows that at some point during the competition his nemesis will try to sabotage his luscious mustache.

What Dargoth doesn't know is that, due to lack of sleep and all this stress he has been going through, hairs have been falling out of his mustache like crazy. The spectators notice this as they go to his booth. They can see the hairs piling up on Dargoth's stout belly. Dargoth doesn't realize this is happening to him. He also doesn't realize all the people leaving his booth, sulking away from him with sad, disappointed looks on their faces. Dargoth doesn't notice because he is too busy spying on Ravengraves with a watchful eye.

Baron Van Ravengraves does not know that Dargoth is eying him from across the fairground. He doesn't even know that his mustache has been shaved off and replaced with a fake drawn-on mustache. He is having too much fun with his friends and fans to pay attention to these things. This is Baron's first mustache competition, so he doesn't quite understand the etiquette involved. For instance, he doesn't know that he is supposed to be standing perfectly still and posed. He moves his head all over the place while talking to his friends and shaking hands with the people that come to his booth. With this attitude, Baron has no chance of winning best in show even if his mustache wasn't a fake.

Dargoth kicks himself for going through so much trouble sabotaging the young vampire. He didn't need to defeat Baron. Baron would have defeated himself!

Lars Van Broadchin

On the other side of the lot, in the far corner of the festival, behind all the food vendor's carts and merry-go-rounds, Rococo sits patiently in his booth with all the other toothbrush mustached contestants.

Not many spectators venture to this section of the fairground, but Rococo is just happy to be a part of the whole event. He has never been a part of anything in his whole life. This makes him feel special, like he is having a birthday party.

Lars Van Broadchin, Baron's vampire friend, finds himself on this side of the festival while wandering around with a giant rainbow lollipop in his mouth. He stops by Rococo's table to compliment

him on his mustache and then they have a little chat about how excited they both are to be there.

Rococo discovers that Lars is actually a very pleasant chap after all, even though their bosses are sworn enemies. You wouldn't think this would be the case with such a scary-looking big bald tattooed character, but he is actually a friendly fun-loving guy.

82

After Lars says goodbye so that he can go see how Baron is doing, Rococo begins to wonder if he has just made a friend. He has never had a friend, so he doesn't know what it is like. He doesn't know if there is some kind of procedure you are supposed to go through before you can call someone your friend.

In any case, it felt good for him to talk to somebody besides Dargoth for a change.

The Melting Mustache

83

After all the spectators have had time to view all of the displays, the judging begins.

The judges enter from the east gate and everyone clears a path for them. These judges are the leading mustachetitions in all of Broodsarrow. They have spent their entire lives studying and theorizing the art of mustachery. Leading the judges is none other than Carlton Van Operaman, who is the most ancient vampire mustachetition in Broodsarrow. He walks with a clipboard in his hands and gets right to work, rating each entry, marking up his papers with checks and stars.

Baron Van Ravengraves is no longer chatty with his friends. He has put on his serious face and

is even trying to come up with a last minute pose. Baron had no idea the judging would be this scary. He is worried that he won't do as good as he had planned. He is worried that the judges won't rate him highly.

He worries so much, in fact, that his pale vampire skin begins to sweat. This sweat moistens his fake mustache, melting it slowly down his face.

84

By the time the judges arrive at his booth, half of his fake mustache has melted onto his upper lip. Operaman notices something suspicious about the young vampire's mustache right away. He rubs his pinky finger under Baron's nose and the makeup smudges into a black blob.

Operaman shakes his head at the first-time contestant.

"Disqualified!" he shouts.

The spectators moan at Baron with dismay and disbelief. Never in the history of mustache competitions has anyone been disqualified for entering a fake mustache.

Ravengraves and all of his friends are in just as much shock as the rest of the crowd. It was a real mustache just yesterday, wasn't it? What happened? Where did it go?

The Faggiest Vampire

It is so baffling to the young vampire that he doesn't suspect Dargoth had anything to do with it. He thinks there must be some kind of mistake. But the judges do not discuss the matter with Baron. They move quickly to the next booth to get away from the stink of a dirty rotten cheater.

The Disappearing Mustache

86

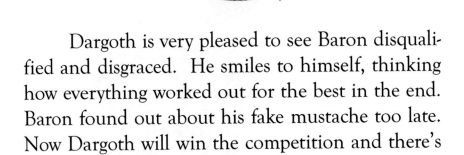

Dargoth is very pleased to see Baron disqualified and disgraced. He smiles to himself, thinking how everything worked out for the best in the end. Baron found out about his fake mustache too late. Now Dargoth will win the competition and there's nothing his young rival can do about it.

Or so Dargoth thinks . . .

Only five booths away from being judged, Dargoth notices something unusual about his mustache. It feels much lighter than normal and his upper lip is getting cold. Dargoth looks down to discover a pile of mustache hairs on his belly.

The Faggiest Vampire

Upon seeing this, Dargoth's stress level explodes. So much stress goes through his nerves that once his fingers reach up to investigate his mustache, all of the remaining hairs collapse under his touch. His entire mustache just pops and the hairs sprinkle downwards like autumn leaves.

Dargoth panics. He doesn't know what else to do. He picks up the pile of mustache hairs and quickly twists them around in the palm of his hand until they become a matted ball. With that ball of hair, he rolls it against the table until it thins into a crayon-shaped tube. Then, believe it or not, he puts this horrid clump of fur underneath his nose and holds it there by puckering his lips as hard as he can.

87

The judges nearly fall over when they come to Dargoth's booth. With his kissy puckering lips, his scraggly crayon-shaped mustache, and his eyebrows raised high on his forehead, the judges assume that Dargoth is playing some kind of joke on them. This was a bad move for Dargoth to make.

If you don't know any mustachetitions, let me tell you that they take mustachery very seriously. They do not like jokes where mustaches are concerned, especially during a very important competition.

Dargoth has just committed the single most disre-spectful offense that any mustache competition has ever endured. And from a champion no less!

"Disqualified!" says Carlton Van Operaman.

Dargoth holds his chest as tight as he can so that his heart doesn't break in there.

Operaman shakes his head at the fallen cham-pion.

"Disgraceful," says the mustachetition.

88

Dargoth falls out of his seat and cowers under-neath his table. He doesn't understand what has happened to his mustache. He doesn't know how such a thing could possibly happen.

Then he thinks about Baron Van Raingraves. Baron comes from a future world filled with fancy gizmos and high technology. Surely Baron must own some kind of gizmo that can make a man's mustache hair fall out from thirty feet away, just by pushing a button.

All this *has* to be Baron's doing. Dargoth will get back at him for this.

Rococo's Change

Rococo is sitting patiently on the other end of the fairground when he begins to change. He didn't realize it before, but this whole time something strange has been happening to his body. Ever since he was bitten by Doomstorm the bulldog, Rococo has been turning into a vampire.

But Rococo isn't turning into just any vampire. Due to the large amount of happiness Rococo has been radiating, something unique and wonderful has been added to the changing process. Something that is turning him into an exceptionally faggy vampire, a kind that The Land of Broodsarrow has never before seen.

A big bright smile is plastered across Rococo's

face. He doesn't know what is happening to him, even as fangs grow down over his bottom lip, he just knows that he feels absolutely splendid and has overwhelmingly good feelings about this competition.

90

As the judges enter the toothbrush mustache section of the fairgrounds, Carlton Van Operaman can already sense a very special mustache before him. A mustachetition as distinguished as he can always sense the presence of a special mustache before it even comes into view.

The brilliance shining out of Rococo's smile has somehow effected the appearance of his mustache, turning his ordinary toothbrush mustache into a luminous golden halo.

As soon as Carlton Van Operaman sees this angel of a mustache, he can't help but fall to his knees and cry tears of joy.

The Heavenly Mustache

Baron Van Ravengraves, having finally realized who was behind his melting mustache, is standing face-to-face with the furious Dargoth Van Gloomfang.

Both vampires have lost everything—their reputations, their fagginess, their mustaches—and all they have left is the possible satisfaction of defeating their opponent. No more tricks and treachery. These two plan to fight it out with their bare fists, right here at the mustache festival, until one of them admits defeat.

Oh, how far these once-noble men have fallen! Resorting to violence is the least honorable, least faggy way to settle a dispute. Never could I have

imagined that either of these gentlemen could sink so low. But here they are in their final act of desperation.

But before either vampire can swing a single punch, something happens . . .

Carlton Van Operaman announces the winner of the mustache competition. This distracts Baron and Dargoth, because they recognize the name of the winner and are positive there has been some sort of mistake.

92

They don't believe it until they see it and even then they are pretty confused.

Rococo is carried on a pedestal through the fairground, his heavenly mustache shining with golden light. All who see this wonderful mustache feel happy inside. The warm heavenly light of the mustache fills the spectators with goodness and delight.

Even Baron and Rococo's grumpy master, Dargoth, are filled with happiness when they look upon the mustache. This glorious sight calms their nerves and they forget all about their trivial complaints.

This magnificient little mustache has brought new light and hope to the ever-gloomy land of Broodsarrow.

Rococo's Party

94

After the mustache competition, Dargoth and Baron decide to congratulate Rococo by throwing him a huge surprise party at Dargoth Castle.

When Rococo enters holding his grand prize ribbon, he jumps in disbelief as he sees that everyone from the entire town is here. Not only did they come to his party, but they are all wearing his party hats! His wonderful, colorful party hats! He smiles so wide that it causes his mustache to beam even brighter than before!

It is a grand celebration that lasts the entire night. There is dancing, singing, and cake. Doomstorm the vampire bulldog even does a backflip of joy!

Dargoth, wearing the crumpled party hat his servant made him, apologizes to Rococo for being such an unfaggy vampire over the past few days.

"You, Rococo," he says. "You are now the faggiest of all faggy vampires. You are the faggiest there ever has been!"

96

Indeed, Rococo *is* the faggiest vampire. In just a single day, he went from being a nobody to a somebody. He went from having his dreams crushed to having his dreams come alive. He went from being nobody's friend to everybody's friend. All this because he always kept his spirits high.

That is the moral of this story, kids. No matter how many people try to stomp on your happiness, you have the power to do whatever you want with your life.

Who knows, perhaps, someday, if you think really happy thoughts as much as you can, the next faggiest vampire might even be . . .

The Faggiest Vampire

98

YOU!

99

THE END

ABOUT THE AUTHOR

Carlton Mellick III's favorite flavor of ice-cream is Mountain Huckleberry, his favorite pizza toppings are pineapple and jalapeno, his favorite color is green, his favorite time of year is early October, and his favorite thing to do is write books. He also likes to draw pictures and breakdance. Sometimes he just likes to sit around and play video games, too.

Lightning Source UK Ltd.
Milton Keynes UK

174192UK00006B/91/P